GODDESS REVEALED

JAY HARTLOVE

TABLE OF CONTENTS

1

WHY A RESEARCH COMPENDIUM?

WELCOME TO *GODDESS REVEALED*. This short volume is a companion to the "Goddess Rising" trilogy, made up of *Goddess Chosen*, *Goddess Daughter*, and *Goddess Rising*, published by Paper Angel Press in August 2019, December 2019, and April 2020. Here I will share with you the fruits of over twenty years of research that went into the books. Indeed, the research that goes into most books forms the vast bulk of the iceberg of time spent writing a book, as compared to the tiny visible ice above water which is the published volume. The research behind these books grew as new facts led to new questions. Historical details fell into place better than I expected, which goaded me into digging deeper. By the time I was done, I had built a secret world behind our own, visible usually only through religious ecstasy. The secrets of that hidden world drive the thrills of the stories, both good and bad.

If most books have a ton of research behind them that supports the author's ability to tell the story but never gets shared with an audience, why do I want to share my research with you?

You don't have to take my word for it. Kirkus Reviews described *Goddess Chosen* saying, "Hartlove fashions a riveting blend of history, religion, and horror in this briskly paced opener. The author balances his ferocious imagination with historical passion. A masterful historical fantasy that informs as well as enthralls." Wouldn't you like a peek behind the curtain?

First of all, I want to thank all my beta readers, fact checkers, and subject matter experts for their immeasurable help in getting these facts correct. The details listed here took me over twenty years to gather. Without their help, I might never have finished.

The "Goddess Rising" trilogy is a supernatural thriller series set in modern times but hinging on events in ancient times. Each book is a stand-alone novel, and together the three tell a larger story arc. Each book is a thriller, with nearly non-stop action, exotic locations, and lots of disturbing twists.

The books are set in our real world, in actual times and locations. My research included what was happening in those locations at the times of the story. The plot tucks in between real-world events to create a secret history.

Technology was also an interesting challenge. The stories take place in 2001, 2004, and 2009. Personal computer and cell phone technology was changing rapidly during this time, and I needed to be sure the consumer tech my characters used reflected the times. Improving communications technology also meant characters could exchange information more efficiently as the stories moved ahead in time.

THE MAGIC IS ALREADY HERE

To tell this story, I needed to introduce magic into our real world. This required coming up with a consistent system of magic the reader can follow, and which makes sense for the characters who are living with it. Since the story is set in our history, the magic is all based on religions found on Earth. With so many religions around the world, I took on the daunting task of finding how they are related and how they connect with one another. The story starts with the religions of the ancient Egyptians and Hebrews, but rapidly moves to Haitian Voodoo, Anglicanism, Korean Cheondogyo, Catholicism, Tibetan Buddhism, and Celtic Druidism.

Yes, you heard that right. The books outline a Unified Field Theory for religion on Earth that reveals the presence of magic. Operating within those rules, I introduce magic into our world and have it work within whatever real-world context and circumstance the story requires.

I want to make an important distinction. Book genre categories are labels authors and publishers use to try to find the right audience. They are buzz words that readers will recognize so they can find the books they want to read. I call these books supernatural thrillers because the protagonists discover the existence of magic and that upsets their understanding of the world. Magic breaks the laws of Physics. It is shocking and often frightening. There is another sub-genre of Fantasy called Urban Fantasy. In those stories, the protagonist often is aware of the existence of magic and knows how to deal with it. The setting is Earth-like and familiar to the reader, but werewolves, vampires, wizards, and witches all blend into those familiar settings. In my books, the unveiling of magic adds to the ever-increasing danger that drives them as thrillers.

Since my research brought me to develop a map for how the world's religions fit together to reveal magic, it made sense to tell these stories around the revelation of magic. Before I tell you how I connected all of this, let me give you some context by taking you a short tour of what happens in the books.

2

SYNOPSES

GODDESS CHOSEN

GODDESS CHOSEN STARTS IN ANCIENT EGYPT, in the court of Ramses the Great, right after the biblical book of Exodus. The Bible tells us that during Exodus, after Moses repeatedly brought down God's miracles to convince Ramses to let the Hebrews free, "Pharoah's heart was hardened." It also tells us that every miracle Moses demonstrated was dismissed by the Egyptian High Priest Janus as nothing more than what the Egyptians already knew how to do. So I ask, who was this Janus who could turn his king's heart and ensure that the king would overplay his hand and lead Egypt to not only lose the Hebrews work force, but also suffer the loss of his best soldiers and embarrassment to the world? In my telling of the tale, the High Priest, whose real name was Nebwebenef, was in fact the Hebrew demon Prince of Liars, the fallen archangel Sammael, the serpent from the Garden of Eden, who would later become known as Lucifer.

Too late, the Egyptian goddess Isis realizes how badly Ramses and the Egyptians were duped and chooses a champion to avenge them. She chooses to reincarnate the successor High Priest, named Royarna, the fellow who had to clean up the mess left after his master disappeared. She reincarnates Royarna as Silas Alverado one hundred generations later, in the 20th century, and sets him on a mission to capture Sammael.

The magic with which Sammael matched all of God's miracles was seen in the Egyptian temple by the highest adapts. He planted that knowledge so that Moses would look insignificant and could be dismissed. Indeed, Sammael is the only creature that could capture the secrets of creation in a form a human mind could understand. These keys were a set of seven images known as the Tablets of Aeth. As soon as Ramses failed spectacularly, Sammael took back the images and disappeared. Silas's mission is to not only capture Sammael, his old treacherous master, but to extract from him these images as revenge, thus gaining the keys to creation. Silas has in mind to use them to solve the world's ills. He also has in mind bringing back the glory that was Egypt, including destroying all other religions, which is essentially the biblical End of Times. Silas is hellbent and utterly ruthless in his quest. He is the apparent villain of the book. I send him on a "hero's journey" to collect what he needs from around the world. The book's cover tag line is, "The man who would beat the devil isn't a hero, but a ruthless madman."

By the time Egypt fell to the Romans a thousand years after Exodus, the religion of Egypt had spread and morphed into local versions all across Africa. Two thousand years later, Europeans kidnapped people from west Africa and brought them to the New World as slaves. In particular, people from Benin were brought to Haiti. The Christian missionaries tried to convert them, but they adapted their faith into Christian imagery and names, forming a new religion called Voodoo. The gods of Voodoo line up deity for deity to the pantheon of ancient Egypt. They are the same gods, living now in a different context.

Silas has in mind to convert the Haitians back to his ancient religion by removing the Christian influences and exposing the true identity of the gods. In this fashion he will have followers ready to worship the gods when he brings them back with the Tablets of Aeth.

The hero of the story is a former Haitian death squad member named Charles Redmond. He was given asylum and a new identity in the United States for giving evidence against his former bosses the Duvaliers. He comes to psychiatrist Sanantha Mauwad, the detective of the series, who is also from Haiti and a Voodoo practitioner, with tales of a demon client. She thinks he is delusional, but when he turns out to be right, she is pulled into the supernatural adventure. Charles's scary client is Joseph, an archangel of the Egyptian pantheon and right-hand muscle for Silas Alverado. Charles hates himself for what he did to the Haitian villagers, regardless of whether he was under orders. When he finds out Silas has in mind to convert the Haitians to the religion of ancient Egypt, which will extinguish Charles's beloved Voodoo, he makes it his quest to stop Silas. As Sammael discovers Silas's plan, he takes advantage of Charles's enthusiasm, which leads to a very tough moral dilemma. Would you side with the Devil to stop a man who would use the Devil's secrets to end civilization as we know it and replace it with his madman utopia?

GODDESS DAUGHTER

The next book, *Goddess Daughter*, is a medical thriller. Sanantha Mauwad is again the detective. A scientist named Randolph Macklin comes to her with a four-month memory gap. The more he learns of what happened then, the more confusing things become. Critics wondered what I was up to making such a sudden turn and not picking up where *Goddess Chosen* left off. These books are self-contained stories, but I needed to fill in a lot of cosmology for the series. Randolph is a leading geneticist who makes a breakthrough in gene therapy, the use of viruses to insert genetic material to repair inherited diseases.

His wife died in a car accident while she was working in Malaysia. Randolph and his teenaged daughter Desiree flew to Malaysia, where Randolph's life-long friend and business partner Young Nae Yoon also lives. That's where Randolph's memories stop. Desiree was bitten by a snake which put her in a coma. Randolph fell into depression and drank himself into a stupor for four months. Young Nae took care of him, waiting for him to come to his senses. But when Randolph sobers up, he can't recall anything of the four months. Sanantha knows this is not normal, so she helps him investigate.

Nothing we learn in the first third of the book turns out to be true. Lies within lies, secrets within secrets, create a puzzle with horrifying answers. Without giving away the mystery, Randolph's science has been used for human cloning. The story explores the nature of evil at a depth even I did not expect. I'm rather proud of how shocking the evil is in this story. I've always wanted to see someone go there, so I went there with my eyes open.

I have filled the book with unnerving coincidences like how tetrodotoxin is used to sap people's will to create zombie slaves in Haiti, but is eaten as a thrilling delicacy in fugu sushi. We also see how martial arts and religion can be combined to create lethal *chi* magic that looks an awful lot like the magic Silas wielded in *Goddess Chosen*.

The story hinges on the intersection of life and souls. The cover tag line is, "How far can you genetically alter someone before she becomes someone else ... before she loses her soul?" This is why Sanantha's spiritualism and Voodoo, combined with her scientific mind, become essential to solving the mystery. By the end of the story, we see how the evil may have been influenced by our old villain Sammael, and how the gods of Egypt/Haiti, in particular Isis/Erzulie, are crucial to saving Desiree's life.

GODDESS RISING

Desiree Macklin turns out to the heroine of the series. Having survived the cloning disaster of the second book, she is reborn and enlivened by the goddess Isis. *Goddess Daughter* is Desiree's origin story; *Goddess Rising* is where Isis picks up after the end of *Goddess Chosen*. In *Goddess Chosen*, Isis reincarnated Royarna to defeat Sammael. He succeeds in capturing the demon, but at the opening of *Goddess Rising*, we see Sammael escape. Isis knew the demon would free himself, so she stepped into Desiree's body when the girl was left with no soul in the cloning gone wrong. Desiree is now her avatar on Earth. If you want something done right, do it yourself.

Goddess Rising opens with Desiree meeting a ghostbuster named Alec Doogan, who has recreated the potion that we first saw Silas use that condenses willpower into action. She then meets Joseph who was set free at the end of *Goddess Chosen*.

Joseph recognizes that Desiree is walking around with the soul of his goddess Isis. Add to this a mysterious benefactor named Benito Nomini supporting Alec's work. Also, Sanantha flies to Ireland to protect Desiree from Joseph. As Benito's role grows more suspicious, a government agent named Michael Archibald comes investigating. While ghostbusting Saint Patrick's gravesite, Alec and Desiree find evidence of angelic intervention. With Benito's help, Alec moves from detecting soul energies to actually performing magic. Meanwhile, Sanantha falls in love with Benito.

You can see where all of this is going. Benito is Sammael. I knew I couldn't hide his identity from the reader, so I reveal him pretty early on, but keep his identity completely hidden from the protagonists in the story. The reader spends the book yelling, "But he's right there!" Michael turns out to be the archangel Michael, the one who threw Lucifer out of heaven. He's back to capture his brother now that Sammael has surfaced to commit mayhem. Once they get passed their historical animosity, Michael and Joseph team up to track down Sammael, which takes some doing since the thing Lucifer is best at is deceit.

Along the way, we confirm that *chi* energy is the same as the soul, and that the condenser fluid bridges the gap between the spiritual and the physical. *Chi* energy is the same as the power the angels wield as magic. The Holy Spirit is *chi*, and is God's gift to mankind to be able to tap angelic power.

The team also picks up a Buddhist monk and a magical pearl that shows the holder the unvarnished truth. We come to see that all these pieces are being moved together by Isis as she devises her trap for Sammael. She is still on her revenge quest from thirty-two hundred years earlier. The cover tag line of the book is, "Saved by a goddess ... but only as a tool for revenge?"

3

INSPIRATION AND RESEARCH

THE STORY BEHIND THE STORY

S OMETIMES FATE HANDS YOU A SITUATION that is just too good to ignore. Thirty-something years ago I was watching Cecil B. DeMille's *The Ten Commandments* for the umpteenth time, and it dawned on me that Moses and Ramses could have sorted out their differences if they hadn't been egged into do-or-die conflict by the people around them. I realized DeMille had made Queen Nefertari an unrelenting shrew to help the male-dominated audience identify with Ramses' conflicts. But it was the role of the head priest at the River Runs Red sequence that got me thinking. So I went to the Bible and looked up how this priest, named Janus by King James' scholars, had stepped in after every one of Moses' miracles and tried to prove that God's acts were nothing more than magical feats already known to the Egyptian temple.

I thought, who this is the guy who gave Ramses the ammo to challenge Moses' god? If Moses' miracles were just Egyptian magic with Jewish special effects, then why should Ramses give an inch on the slavery issue? And if this priest played such a deal-killing role and still stayed in the background, maybe he was Really Dangerous. Maybe he was the Devil. I got writing.

I had already gathered a number of elements for a story about a guy who goes to a psychiatrist railing on about a demon, which turns out to be real. It was a natural fit to plug these two stories together, with the Ramses story as background for the demon story today. I hammered away for a while to get it all to fit together. I decided the demon in the psychiatrist story was actually a different demon from the priest in the Ramses story, but otherwise it all fell together without too much hand wringing.

So I get though a draft, having purposely made all the dates and names fuzzy to avoid hate mail from Egyptologists and religious experts. Armed with a story that worked and characters I liked, I was ready to face the ugly reality of history and all the facts that I assumed would push my story out of the realm of possibility and into the realm of fantasy. Boy, was I in for a surprise.

RESEARCH TOPICS

I had three areas that needed research: Haitian Voodoo, Ancient Egyptian magic, and the origin of the Tarot. All three turned out to have endless caverns of raw data. Now mind you, this was in 1988 before the advent of the Internet or search engines. So I went digging. I was determined that even if my story would end up outside of history, I should get the details right. I wanted to know what life was like in the Egyptian temple. I wanted to know what it was like to witness a Voodoo loa mounting. I read everything I could find. I went to New Orleans to learn about Voodoo. I scoured occult bookstores for the history of the Tarot. I went to the British Museum to learn about Ancient Egypt. As I learned more, I filled in the details in the book. The settings and characters grew richer with this background. And since I hadn't found anything directly contradictory to the plot, I kept the story as I had originally conceived it.

In the meantime, my personal life went to the dogs. I ended up in a divorce with money troubles, and the enthusiasm for getting the book published just languished. But the research sustained me, and I kept reading.

So years go by, I recover from my slump, and I meet and marry a wonderful woman. On our honeymoon, I find myself walking through the British Museum, giving my new wife a personal tour of the mummy cases, the jewelry and the statuary, having a grand time seeing all of the stuff I had just spent the last nine years reading about. We were in the Grand Gallery looking at the rose granite colossus bust of Ramses II, and I noticed that the curators have surrounded the king with statues of his wives, relatives and priests. His priests? I checked the dates. My story postulates that after the Exodus incident, Ramses' High Priest escaped up river into ancient Kush, and the successor High Priest, who is left to pick up the pieces, is my antagonist. To my utter amazement, the statues showed that there was indeed a change in the post of High Priest of Amun fifteen years into Ramses's reign.

WRITING ABOUT REAL PEOPLE

Suddenly I was writing about real people. I marched into the museum bookstore and found every name reference and chronology they had. Nebwenenef was the first priest, who joined Ramses' court right after Ramses ascended to the throne in 1279 BCE. He left the post in 1263 BCE, which is a perfectly acceptable date for the Exodus. (More on this in a later chapter.) Royarna (often simply Roy) took over as the new High Priest of Amun. This was too good to be true. But if I were going to use these real historical men, I would have to get the details absolutely correct.

I took my new research and returned to the writing desk with revived gusto. While I was at it, I fleshed out my modern characters' back stories to match my ancient ones. I filled in Silas' youthful encounter with the Nazis and Charles' background with the Duvaliers. Soon there were enough historical touchstones that those places where I did have to distort history to fit the story were in the minority.

Those of you who have read *Goddess Chosen* may have spotted the few places where I stretched history. To get the Voodoo pantheon to line up with the gods worshipped during the reign of Ramses II, I had to move the Cult of Isis back several hundred years. I used Herodotus' rather fanciful description of the subterranean tunnels of the Necropolis, even though he wrote

800 years after the Exodus. I am fully aware that the Tarot deck was developed in Eastern Europe in Medieval times. But who am I not to take advantage of the mistake the Renaissance Western Europeans made in thinking the Gypsies of Romania were the descendants of the ancient Egyptians? (More on this in the Tarot chapter.) Entire New Age movements are based on the notion that the Tarot was developed by the ancient Egyptians. Who am I to say otherwise?

I also appreciate that I pushed the envelope, although only a little, on nerve trigger thresholds and cortical processing of visual information when Silas interrogates Security Chief Bailey. My intent was to creep you out while demonstrating Silas' determination to get what he wants.

Lastly, I certainly know that Nebwenanef does not mean "name not spoken". Egyptian history gives us precedent for stricken names and what better place for one to show up than the embarrassing loss in Exodus? I apologize to the descendants, scholars, and other fans of Nebwenanef for casting this very respectable man as the Devil in disguise.

EXODUS, ROY, AND NEBWENENEF

A favorite quest of archeologists is to match religious accounts to historical records. One of the most frustrating non-matches is the story of Exodus. The simple explanation for the complete lack of historical record of this momentous event is that the Egyptians were the only ones in a position to write about it, and they were too embarrassed at the loss. Many researchers have taken the mismatch as evidence that other key dates in the popularly accepted chronology of the ancient world are indeed wrong. There was an exodus in Assyria, but eight hundred years earlier. And many of the acts attributed to Moses are in fact traceable to Elijah 300 years later. The biblical dating puts the Exodus in the year 1447 BCE, 200 years earlier than the reign of Ramses II. The problem with pinning down dates is unfortunately inherent in the nomadic, unsettled nature of the Jewish people during this time.

WILL THE REAL EXODUS PHARAOH PLEASE STAND UP?

By far the most popular choice for Exodus Pharaoh is Ramses II, despite history, because the Bible calls him Ramesses. Ramses the First had a very short reign, and I haven't seen anyone suggest that it could have been him. Ramses II had a son who succeeded him to the throne for ten years, named Merenptah. Merenptah's son was crowned as Ramses III, and his reign is also well-documented. Ramses II is known to have used prisoners of war from Canaan as slave labor. He had expanded Egypt's imperial borders all the way into modern day Lebanon. And although his popularity with his people stemmed largely from his military conquests (as George S. Patton put it, "People love a winner."), history shows that he was impulsive and often made huge errors in battle strategy. This sounds a lot like the guy in the Bible.

The historical record points to another king, Thutmose III, who ruled from 1504 to 1450 BCE. The Jewish calendar dates the Exodus at 1447 BCE. There are several Egyptian accounts of cosmic cataclysm — darkness, fire falling from the sky — written later about events in Thutmose's reign. Pumice from the titanic explosion of the Aegean island of Thera has been found in Egypt and dated to this time as well. The explosion of Thera, by far the biggest volcanic explosion in recorded history, provides a number of explanations for the Ten Plagues in Exodus. The boils could be from acid rain, the darkness could be from the ash clouds, the parting of the Red (Reed) Sea could easily be accomplished from tidal backwash of the tsunami that ripped the entire Mediterranean Sea. Of course, all of these events would have happened within hours of one another, not across the span of days as described in the Bible. Not to mention that more accurate radiocarbon dating of the Thera explosion puts it at 1628 BCE, which doesn't line up with any reasonable Exodus Pharaoh candidate.

So given the stubborn mismatches between scientific dating, written historical records, and stories steeped in religious agenda, I chose to stick with the one handy coincidence I had found: that the post of High Priest of Amun changed hands fifteen years into the reign of Ramses II. Unfortunately for my story, Nebwenenef did not disappear suspiciously, but rather died in 1263 BCE. He was buried at Thebes and his tomb is a great source for hymns from the period. Oh well. On the other hand, in my story, Ramses orders his actual name (Faenka) stricken from all records and replaced with the fake name Nebwenenef, which I postulate actually meant "name not spoken", but this meaning has been lost to history. In such an event, the Egyptians in power may well have constructed a tomb and made it look like their beloved High Priest had died, rather than admit to the public that they had let the Exodus culprit get away.

NEBWENENEF AND ROY

What further drew me to Nebwenenef as a supernatural figure was how he came to power. Right after being crowned, Ramses went to Thebes, the major religious center of the day, to give tribute to the gods. As he was leaving, the oracle of Amun, the sun god and the leader of their pantheon, told Ramses that Nebwenenef had been hand-picked by Amun to be High Priest. Ramses immediately consented, and Nebwenenef went straight from local bishop to head of the church. In this period, the High Priests of Amun had great power and were given great wealth. They were essentially allowed to rule Upper Egypt (the southern part) and were even sometimes given the title "king."

Now if you were the Hebrew demon Prince of Liars and you wanted to lay the groundwork for a fifteen-year plan to ruin your enemy's king, what better place to start than to pull a supernatural string or two and get yourself installed as the head of their church, in charge of all of your enemy's learning and magic?

Roy died during the reign of Ramses' son, Merenptah, and was probably Merenptah's High Priest as well. He was buried on the west bank of the Nile at Thebes at Dra' Abu al-Naja in the Valley of the Kings, in the back of the large Ramesseum. His tomb was restored in the late 1990s. It's small, but exquisitely painted with scenes of feasts and funerals and worship. As to his succession to the post of High Priest, again we are faced with the maddening mismatch of dates. Depending on whose dating you use, Ramses II reigned from either 1279 to 1213 BCE or from 1290 to 1224 BCE. This twelve-year discrepancy is bigger than the biggest gap I could find between Nebwenenef's death and Roy's assumption of the post, and I cannot find any mention of any other High Priest in between the two. Up until his assumption to High Priest of Amun, Roy was not only a religious leader, but a highly placed scribe. So even though I can't tell you what date the handover happened, I can tell you I am confident that Roy was the next person to carry the High Priest title after Nebwenenef died.

So my stage was set. At the start of Ramses' reign, his adoptive brother Moses had already been cast out into the desert by Ramses' father Seti I as a traitor. Sammael would know that Moses would be back in a few years to set his people free. Sammael created the Faenka guise and got himself installed as High Priest. Once there, he started introducing more and more powerful magic into the Egyptian temple, being careful to not actually give the Egyptians anything they could keep. When Moses finally returned, Faenka showed Ramses that Moses had nothing beyond what the Egyptians already had. Which made the conflict personal, not cosmological. And given Ramses' record for hot headed overreaction, the result was in the bag. After Ramses lost and the Hebrews got away, Faenka fled with the powerful magic. Ramses struck his name, replacing it with Nebwenenef. Ramses gave Roy the High Priest post and demanded Roy enlist the gods to find the traitor. Too late, Roy and the Isis figured out what happened. One hundred generations later, Isis reincarnated Roy as Silas and sets him on a mission to capture his old master and force him to give up the secrets with which he had once taunted the Egyptians.

SAMMAEL AND THE TABLETS OF AETH

Before one can trace the history of Old Testament demons or angels, one has to realize that the Middle East bred a different kind of deity than we think of today. Geography plays a big role in the gods and monsters that a people concoct to explain their world. Even before the Cedars of Lebanon were cut down to build the Roman navy, and before the grasslands that were Northern Africa were overgrazed by nomadic shepherds into the sandy dustbowl that it is now, the Middle East has always been small pockets of civilization spread apart by huge expanses of inhospitable nothing. Only the most powerful gods were thought to be able to travel vast distances at the speed of thought, or to sit on high and be able to affect any point on the world. The ever-present, all-seeing gods that developed in the East were a reflection of the Eastern notion that everything is interrelated and connected. On the other hand, the Middle East, and later the West, has always been more separated and isolated. It wasn't until Christianity spread into Europe that Westerners abandoned the notion of local gods and started thinking in terms of a God On High.

Other than God/Yahweh/Jehovah, the ancient Jewish supernatural world was populated by creatures that would manifest in an isolated existence, that had to take time to travel from point A to point B, that you could actually run away from, and that you could actually capture. This sets the stage for some very personal interactions where learned men faced unearthly temptations and gained otherworldly knowledge. The tales of these episodes have been cataloged by rabbis who have passed the lessons on to future generations.

These rabbinical tales formed the primary research materials for Christian mystics in Medieval times and since. Just as Christianity teaches that God is everywhere and all-powerful, it is also from its Jewish roots that it gets the concept of angels and devils that show up in one place to interact with individual humans. Such interactions were, of course, the object of all the ceremony that came to be known as the Black Arts.

SAMMAEL

Sammael was the ancient Jewish demon Prince of Liars. He was a fallen angel, the chief of the ten evil Sephiroth, and mate to Lilith, who was Adam's first wife. He was the snake in the Garden of Eden. He was the angel who told Sarah that Abraham had killed their son Issac, upon which false news she died of grief. He was cast out of heaven by the archangel Michael. It wasn't until the founders of the Christian church found they needed a pan-galactic Enemy to go along with their pan-galactic God that the snake from the Garden of Eden was reassigned to become the all-powerful opponent of everything good that we now know as Satan. The arrival of the seemingly world-enveloping Black Plague in medieval times had a lot to do with Sammael (local) becoming the

Devil (omnipresent). In *Goddess Chosen*, I have Sammael amused at how his perceived role in the universe has grown.

Of all the tales of people dealing with, and losing to, Sammael, the one that I cite in the book is about a 15th century Spanish kabbalist. After figuring out how to summon the demon, the magician made a pure gold crown onto which he inscribed the runic words for "Thy master's name is upon thee." He succeeded in coaxing Sammael to appear, at which point he dropped the crown onto the snake's head. Being forced to admit his subservient place, the snake agreed that the magician, in speaking on God's behalf, had captured him. Sammael then convinced the magician to celebrate his success by burning incense. Failing to remember that he was dealing with the Prince of Liars, the magician didn't stop to consider that burning incense is an act of idolatry, which means the magician was no longer speaking for God, which broke the spell. The story doesn't elaborate what Sammael then did to the poor fellow.

4

THE WESTERN MYSTERY TRADITION

ORIGINS OF THE TAROT

B ESIDES RABBINICAL TALES, the other great source of research material for Western mystics is ancient Egypt. Even before Napoleon's armies started dragging statuary back from Egypt, the courts of Europe were aflame with conjecture about the new finds that were being dug out of the sand. The French court of Louis XVI was beset with neo-Egyptian fashions and ceremony. Every con man who could pitch an explanation tried to wend his way into the imaginations of the wealthy who were desperate to tie themselves somehow to ancient grandeur. Of course, no one had translated any of the writing yet (Jean-Francois Champollion's work came after the French Revolution), but that made it all that much more enticing.

In an effort to find anything Egyptian, a lot of incorrect assumptions were made, but a lot of previously disconnected archeology came together. A temple of Serapis (Osirus) in southern

Italy was correctly identified as from the 2nd Century BCE Ptolemaic period, when Romans were adopting and spreading what they had found. The temple had a hall with twenty-two elaborately painted panels that had clearly ceremonial importance. These images were copied and fed into the conjecture mill. Someone then incorrectly tied them to the playing cards used by the fortune-telling forest people of eastern Europe. (Decorated gambling cards go back to the 1400's, and have been outlawed by the Church almost from the start.) Hence these folks were labeled Gypsies, as if they were the long lost descendants of the Egyptians. (They are actually originally from India.) The temple images were put onto cards and were thought to give the user magical powers to tell the future. So, the images of the Tarot deck do have an ancient Egyptian origin, even if we still do not know what those images were used for in the temple.

CAGLIOSTRO AND HIS SUCCESSORS

One of the greatest con men mystics of this period was Giuseppe Balsamo, who styled himself Count Alessandro Cagliostro. He was very bright, very charismatic, and very outspoken. He managed to bring his version of ancient Egyptian civilization to the Louis court and convinced a close friend of Queen Marie Antoinette, a Princess de Lamballe, that she was descended from that revered lineage. He made many friends in high places when he also spoke out against the teachings of the Freemasons, insisting publicly that Elias Ashmole's legend of Hiram and the workers of Salomon's Temple was hogwash. The leaders of the brewing revolution were, of course, Freemasons who used their religious meetings as cover for planning insurrection. His views did not do him any good after the revolution succeeded, and he died in a prison tower.

But his Egyptian Rites lived on spectacularly. A long succession of mystics adopted and modified Cagliostro's original interpretations, carrying on a line of thinking that lasted for the next two centuries. Contemporary adepts included Franz Anton Mesmer (the hypnosis pioneer) and the Comte de Saint-Germain (who may or may not have initiated Cagliostro, and around whom Chelsea Quinn Yarborough wrote a successful series of vampire books). Many combined Freemasonry and the Egyptian Rites, reconciling their differences to create a unified magical theorem. Through the 1800s, this line included Sir Edward Bulwer-Lytton, Alphonse Louis Constant (a.k.a. Eliphas Levi), Dr. Paschal Beverly Randolph, and Madame Helena Blavatsky. This unified magic theorem came to be called the Western Mystery Tradition, and it includes Tarot reading, astrology, crystal gazing, hierarchical initiation ranks, hypnosis (both self and on others), and ritualized communication with the beyond. By the end of the 1800s, several competing groups of mystics had developed, all splintered from this line. The most famous of these was the Hermetic Order of the Golden Dawn. This group counted among its members such luminaries as A. E. Waite (who designed the most widely used modern Tarot deck) and Aleister Crowley. Crowley, like many of the Golden Dawn members, left the order to pursue his own magical research. He claimed to have conquered death before moving to Sicily to found his own mystic colony where drugs and sex flowed freely.

Another of these groups was the Rosicrucians. This group, which today has its headquarters in San Jose, California, went back to its supposed Egyptian roots, incorporating translations and modern scientific views of ancient Egyptian life into their mysticism. Since Cagliostro first introduced the symbol of Thoth's Rose-Cross, the Rosicrucians claim him as one of the founders of their sect.

GROWING A TRADITION

By the 1930s, there was a well-developed view of how ancient Egyptian magic could be used by modern man. Unfortunately, many European adherents were also deeply racist. Former members of the Order of the Golden Dawn and rival groups made sure this magical heritage was incorporated into Nazi German thinking. Among others, Dietrich Eckhart (to whom Hitler dedicated *Mein Kampf*) brought the Thule/Atlantis myth, while Karl Haushofer brought Tibetan ritual and the notion of secret masters. These occultists found eager followers for their views in Joseph Goebbels and Heinrich Himmler. Goebbels, Himmler, and Hitler became fanatical believers that not only were the German people descended from the Aryan conquerors of ancient India, but that the Aryans were the descendants of a race of supermen from a sunken Atlantis-like civilization in the North called Thule. These esoteric views shored up the official racist doctrine founded on hatred for Jews, Slavs, and anything not

German. In *Goddess Chosen*, Silas speaks of how as a young man he tried to talk Goebbels out of this fantasy and to embrace the original faith of ancient Egypt, but to no avail.

Among the inheritors of the Western Mystery Tradition was a Czech mystic named Franz Bardon. Bardon was captured by the Nazis and interrogated for the location of the ninety-nine secret lodges that Hitler believed contained the learning he needed to cement his victory. Bardon told them nothing, outlasted their tortures, and was liberated by Russians. I borrowed freely from Bardon's writings in developing Silas' magic system, which I describe in another chapter here. Bardon was also something of a political activist, which landed him in a Soviet prison, where he died in 1958.

Somewhere along the line, as Cagliostro's magic system matured, it became necessary to surmise the existence of magic that had not yet been found. These mystics had the Tarot, they all had their own versions of how astrology fit with magic, and they had their links to the ancient world. Yet they appreciated — even if only privately — that their magic was largely self-hypnosis and largely ineffectual. Clearly there was something more that had been lost to history. After all, we have these stories of large-scale, public miracles being accomplished in ancient times. And so the search was on to find the missing pieces, which came to be called the Tablets of Aeth. Eventually, all the splinter groups claimed to have found pieces of the Aeth magic. To this day, the Rosicrucians call their innermost teachings the Priesthood of AEth (complete with the odd capitalization).

If this all seems like so much mental masturbation, and that no one really believes any of this stuff, stop and consider some of the rather influential folks who have held these teachings in high regard. I already mentioned the Nazis. The founders of the United States were Freemasons, and to this day U.S. currency is covered with Masonic images. Since Freemasonry is based on a myth tied to Jewish history, it is easily accepted by practicing Christians. Masonic temples stand in plain view in every town in America, which is largely a Christian country. The occult literature of the 20th Century was written almost entirely by folks working from the Freemason/Rosicrucian heritage. This stuff is a part of our cultural landscape.

My contribution to this grand cycle is to tie Sammael to the Exodus, and to tie them both to Tarot magic, and make the Tablets of Aeth the long-lost Tarot cards with which Sammael suckered the ancient Egyptians.

SILAS' MAGIC

Serious Egyptologists are going to hate what I have propounded as ancient Egyptian magic, not because it doesn't feel right, but because of my sources. They will have every right to be upset. To them I apologize, but with a caveat: I have seen what has been pieced together of authentic ancient Egyptian ritual and, aside from some amusing masturbation ceremonies, it is mind-numbingly dry. Everything is built around begging the gods to intervene. Nowhere is the command over nature that I needed to give Silas. On the other hand, I have shown Silas' rituals to serious students of ancient Egypt who are somehow completely unfamiliar with the Western Mystery Tradition, only to have them tell me the stuff looks great, but then ask where I found it. The answer is also the answer to why I made this choice: the stuff is all around us and it feels like magic because our culture is steeped in it.

The founders of America and the planners of the French Revolution organized their concepts at an auspicious time when the mysteries of ancient Egypt were just being unearthed. As these finds where quickly snatched up and assimilated by occultists, a tradition developed that included hierarchical initiation ranks and symbols of personal power. Leaders across the West adopted this tradition because it lent legitimacy through attachment with the glorious past. Science had not yet filled in the details of ancient Egyptian life, so the occultists filled the growing need. By the time translations had been made of enough carvings and paintings to piece together what life was really like so long ago, the Mystery Tradition, which was supposed to have been the ancient ways, had developed into something very different. Very few people took the time to stay abreast of the facts unveiled by science, but everyone knew the symbols their leaders had adopted from the Mystery Tradition.

By the way, the spell that Silas casts at the end of *Goddess Chosen* to capture Sammael is not Western Mystery Tradition; it's the actual ancient Egyptian rite of creation.

And the 130-foot yacht dubbed *The Purgatory* that Silas uses as his base of operations was in fact the flagship of the Westport line in 2001 when this story is set. It is big enough to meet his needs, but still agile enough to outrace a tsunami shockwave. That math was a lot of fun.

WORKING WITH WHAT THEY HAD

In defense of the drafters of the Western Mystery Tradition (hereinafter "WMT"), I have to point out they were not working in a complete vacuum. Greek writers had chronicled life in Egypt as its empire fell to Rome. These writings had been studied extensively in the West throughout Medieval and Renaissance times. When the physical evidence showed up, and seemed to match the long-studied writings, the writings were deemed accurate. But long before the French dug Karnak out of the sand, occultists had already been working to assimilate the Greek writings into their philosophical systems. When the Greek writings were legitimized by the diggings, so too was the body of apocryphal work that had been attached to the Greek writings. Suddenly it became difficult to separate facts that had been observed in 200 C.E. and 14th Century conjecture based on Greek writings.

Even today it's difficult to parse out specific details. Some trustworthy sources directly contradict other trustworthy sources — and on sometimes major details. Historians enamored of Cagliostro say he was a royalist, while others enamored of his supposed mentor the Comte de Saint-Germain claim Cagilostro was among the founders of the French Revolution. The British Museum has Roy cataloged as a High Priest of Amun during the early 19th Dynasty, while the folks who restored his tomb in Dra' Abu al-Naja identify him as only a highly placed scribe, and at the end of the 18th Dynasty. One disturbing thing I have found in my research is that history is not only an incomplete patchwork, but it is very much colored by the vagaries and biases of the people who pieced it together.

So, as an author trying to paint a complete and believable picture, I had to make choices among the options I found in the research. Since the WMT had evolved alongside what we now have as Western Civilization, it made sense from the readership's viewpoint to start there instead of starting with hieroglyphic translations. Better to give the reader images that ring familiar while telling a complex story than to risk burying the story in unfamiliar, but accurate, scientific details. And I was careful to insert plenty of modern scientific findings along the way.

FRANZ BARDON

I set out to find a WMT occultist who presented a simple, but complete magic system from which I could use powerful images that would ring true to a Western audience. I didn't have to look very far. Franz Bardon was born in 1909 in Troppau (now Opava), Czechoslovakia. He began showing aptitude for esoteric studies at the age of fourteen. Prior to the outbreak of WWII, he performed stage magic under the name Frabato (FRAnz-BArdon-Troppau-Opava) while making his living as an industrial mechanic. In 1945, near the end of the war, he was captured by the Nazis and interrogated for the location of secret lodges where occult masters supposedly held magical knowledge the Nazis wanted. In swallowing the Thule-Atlantis myth, Hitler had also come to believe the Thule masters had preserved their teachings in some ninety-nine secret lodges around the world. Bardon was known to be an accomplished occultist with many connections with other occultists, so when Germany conquered Czechoslovakia, they came after Bardon. He didn't tell them anything, managed to live through their tortures, and was rescued from prison by invading Russian soldiers. After the war, he made his living as a natural healer, and taught Hermetics.

In 1956, he wrote his first treatise, "An Initiation Into Hermetics". It is a ten-step, hands-on course in how to train yourself to be a magician. No kidding. One of the refreshing things about reading Bardon is his frankness. He flatly claims that he wouldn't write anything that he hadn't done himself. His symbols are clearly from the WMT: the Magus Crown, the dagger of command, the wand of willpower, the use of magic mirrors. Some of his finer defining details are adapted from previous WMT practitioners. In particular, his "condenser fluids" concept looks a lot like Paschel Beverly Randolph's electrical-sexual energies. I love how these guys refined their predecessors' work. What is different about Bardon is his utterly stripped down, completely practical presentation. Gone are the Golden Dawn complexities of astrology. Gone are the Freemason Christian overlays of the Trinity. It's just you the magician, and the universe at your command. Hang on tight.

Also in 1956, Bardon published his second treatise, called "A Practical Guide to Evocation". In it, he instructs the reader how to contact the supernatural plane, and then catalogs all the angels and demons he has communicated with, including their mystical calling symbols. I swear, I'm not making this up.

Bardon's third and last complete treatise, titled "The Key to the True Kabbalah", was written near his death. All three of these books were written in German, and were first translated into English in 1975. This work relies heavily on the first two, and is a much denser read, and so it is not as accessible. In it, Bardon ties together Indian Tantric mysticism, Jewish Kabbalah, and other sources to reveal the nature of the universe in colors, sounds, numbers and vibrations.

In addition to having a Promethean ethic of bringing occult secrets to the masses, he was also politically active. This landed him in a Soviet prison on trumped up tax evasion charges, where he died in 1958.

After his death, Bardon's student and secretary Otti Votavova published *Frabato the Magician* as an autobiographical fiction, compiled from Bardon's notes.

SILAS ALVERADO

What I borrowed most from Franz Bardon and gave to Silas Alverado was attitude. Silas is on a mission. He knows his magic worked thousands of years ago, and he knows it works now. He unflinchingly picks up his tools and just does whatever has to be done. Bardon's practical rituals are tailor made for this can-do attitude. The principal ceremonies I took from Bardon are the preparation of implements and the summoning of spirits. But since these are central to everything Silas does, I had to be sure all the other magic I gave Silas fit with these rituals, especially the practical, hands-on, can-do feel. Silas has already figured out the astrological aspects of his plan and built a timetable before *Goddess Chosen* starts. As long as he sticks to his schedule, he doesn't have to concern himself with such details. As the story progresses and Sammael comes to suspect what Silas is doing, and acts to stop Silas, Silas needs the hands-on flexibility to improvise.

Silas sees no conflict between his wielding command over nature and his having a solemn reverence for its beauty and elegance. I go to lengths in the Preface to show how the Egyptians saw the world as a hierarchy of perfection. Those at the top could command what was below them, but only if they understood and appreciated it. This is not WMT; this is accurate to what we now understand of ancient Egyptian philosophy. When the Purgatory comes under nuclear attack, Silas demonstrates a knowledge of geology on top of everything else.

I had to make Silas' spells look different enough from what is described in Exodus to support the Sammael hypothesis. The Ten Plagues and the magic Sammael (as Faenka) used to counter the Plagues are only achievable with the Tablets of Aeth. Since these tablets are the ultimate object of Silas' quest, I needed to keep Silas as far as possible from turning sticks into snakes or parting bodies of water. He does summon an army of insects when trapped in a collapsed tomb, but only by asking a god to do it for him.

In constructing Silas' rituals, I liberally used another WMT convention: Cause by Analogy. When Silas needs to contact Osirus, he selects a plane of existence where Osirus' sarcophagus mirrors the glass case back in London that contains Ramses' mummy. What happens in one plane is reflected in the other. When Silas seeks revenge on al-Qabek in Cairo, he builds a model of the antiquities dealer's office building. Setting the model on fire does the same to the building itself. When he possesses Nila's body in the Sudan, he uses a hollow silver bead as a model for her body vessel. When he needs to disable the nuclear missile on the bottom of the Atlantic, he aims his spell at his crewman's watch.

Hypnosis also plays no small role in Silas' tool bag. He hypnotizes Bailey to get the museum alarm details. He hypnotizes himself to regress into his previous self to read the deteriorated tomb painting. Self-hypnosis is central to the narrowed-focus, no-self trance state used in almost all magic, WMT, Eastern or any other.

5

THE VOODOO CONNECTION

HAITI AND VOODOO

SILAS ALVERADO CHOOSES TO START his reinstatement of the gods of ancient Egypt in Haiti because Voodoo is the inheritor descendant of that ancient religion.

When the Romans took over Egypt, and forced their versions of the Greek gods into widespread use, the Egyptian gods went underground and became the animus gods of Western Africa. These gods are personal gods who take possession of people to work their influence on the world. From what we have pieced together of the worship practices of ancient Egypt, there was a lot of role playing of the gods by priests. I postulate that the gods of ancient Egypt possessed their devotees, and continued to do so in West Africa.

Fast forward two thousand years to the 17th Century, when European slave traders kidnapped the Yoruba people from the Ivory Coast and take them to the Caribbean to work on plantations. While there, these displaced animus believers were indoctrinated by

Christian missionaries. They adapted and blended the two religions into what is now called Voodoo. Voodoo has a Savior, a Virgin Mother, and an Father godhead, as well as a host of lesser deities, all of whom can possess people, or ride them in "mountings." This is why Voodouns refer to their gods, or loas as the "Divine Horsemen".

Therefore Voodoo is the descendent and inheritor of two religious traditions that, back in the book of Exodus, were opposed to one another. Judea eventually spawned Christianity, while Egypt eventually spawned the animus faiths. To get back to ancient Egypt, Silas has in mind to start with Voodoo and strip away the Christian influences.

In *Goddess Chosen*, Silas describes how the gods of Egypt are the same as the gods of Voodoo, almost as if their Voodoo identities are disguises. Erzulie is Isis. Legba is Horus. Damballah is Ra. Baron Samedi is Osirus. Joseph says he is an archangel of the god Ptah, and Sanantha deduces that makes him an incarnation of the Voodoo god Guede L'Orange. By calling the gods by their proper names and summoning them with their original rituals, Silas has demonstrated to his converted village that the gods will serve the people even better.

HAITI'S ROUGH START

The island of Hispanola was settled in the 1500s, and slaves were brought in all through the 1600s to grow tobacco and sugar. France and Spain finally settled their ongoing dispute over the island and divided it between them in 1697. After more than a hundred years of French rule, the Haitian people rose up against their French masters and liberated their island in 1804. In fact, they were the only colony of Napoleon's France to break free. Out of this rebellion came tales of how the loas helped the people, and how the people owed the loas for their freedom. (Yellow Fever wiped out a significant number of the French forces.)

After their revolt, the Haitians found themselves without support from the nations of the Caribbean or from America. Their new nation fell into poverty right away when they had to pay France war reparations (equivalent to $21 billion today) in exchange for their sovereignty in 1825. It has never recovered in 200 years.

Such an unrelenting slump has led to cultural explanations. Many Haitians believe their poverty is the revenge their loas have taken for not showing proper thanks for the success of the revolt against France. Others feel that the Haitian people became poor because they rejected hard work once they were free, that hard work was what they had done when they were slaves, and they weren't going to do it anymore.

The real cause has been the exploitation of the natural resources. Haiti is a tropical island and produces cash crops. But it is a very mountainous island, and local warlords have been able to take and keep control for decades at a time. By skimming any wealth out of the economy, no infrastructure has ever been built, education has been suppressed, the trees have all been ripped out, and the people have been kept poor and subservient.

VOODOO

The Voodoo faith itself has developed around this isolated mountainous environment. Each priest is given final authority to interpret the gods' intentions. There are no bishops to appeal to, and no hierarchy to enforce uniformity of doctrine nor liturgy. What your priest says, goes. And if you are unlucky enough to get a corrupt priest, then your village can stay oppressed for a lifetime.

On the other hand, this faith serves the Haitian people very well. They live in isolated valleys where they are torn between the cruelty from their masters (whether domestic or foreign) and the joy of living in a tropical paradise. The loas actually show up at their ceremonies, which gives huge comfort that the gods really do care. Their rituals are immersed in singing and drumming and dancing and the celebration of life. At first, it may even seem a mismatch that a people so oppressed for so long would have such joy in their hearts. But wouldn't you also, if you knew your gods were present and engaged in your affairs?

I was originally concerned about offending modern Voodoo practitioners by having Silas claim this religion is a blending of ancient Egyptian and modern Christian beliefs. But among my research trips, I went to New Orleans, where I met a mambo priestess who told me Voudouns fully understand their religion to be a synthesis of many other religious sources, including Egyptian.

RECENT HISTORY

In 1957, Francois "Papa Doc" Duvalier seized power as President-for-Life and began to systematically siphon off all the wealth the nation had to offer. He used the army to enforce his rule, and some 30,000 Haitians were killed for political reasons over the next 14 years. When Papa Doc died in 1971, he handed power to his son Jean-Claude "Baby Doc" Duvalier, who continued in the office of President-for-Life. He continued his father's reign of terror until 1986, when a military junta finally seized control. This was followed by a succession of alternating presidents and juntas that continues until today.

As news of the atrocities and human rights abuses under Baby Doc finally garnered the American public's attention, the U.S. Government started gathering evidence to bring the Duvaliers to trial. To get this evidence, the U.S. allowed many of Duvalier lieutenants to flee to America. Principal among these was Emanuel "Toto" Constant who came here in 1994. I placed Charles Montrouge as a former member of Constant's paramilitary death squad the Front for the Advancement and Progress of Haiti (FRAPH). When Charles was given asylum and new life in the U.S., he changed his name to Redmond. (Constant was eventually convicted of mortgage fraud in 2008.)

Although this story takes place between January and April of 2001, I hope that my portrayal of the Haitian people as reasonable, capable, and sympathetic will raise some awareness today. A lot of mean-spirited misinformation has been forced on the American public in the wake of the disastrous earthquake that hit Haiti on January 12, 2010, especially about the religion of Voodoo. I would be thrilled if my books can help clear up misconceptions about this vibrant faith that serves its people so well.

6

PLACING THE STORIES IN REAL TIME

HOW THE WORLD HAS CHANGED

T HE FIRST BOOK, *GODDESS CHOSEN*, takes place in early 2001, beginning January 26 and ending on the first day of Passover, which was April 8. I don't have to remind you that history took an abrupt downward turn on September 11, 2001. In *Goddess Chosen*, I make reference to the religious paranoia surrounding the turn of the millennium, which occurred on January 1, 2001. You will recall the world held its breath on January 1, 2000, to see if all the clocks in all the computers would crash. The fear of this potential disaster eclipsed the actual millennium turn a year later. I was writing *Goddess Chosen* all through the 1990s, and I had picked these dates for my brush with apocalypse some time before the date arrived. After 9/11, I was really glad I had picked Spring 2001, since there are so many things in the book that could not happen as I described them since the world's War on Terror began.

The heightened security in places like airports and museums is the principal difference. As clever as Silas and Joseph are in the story, I would have had a lot more work on my hands making it believable to break into the British Museum or to plant bombs on an airplane at Miami International Airport.

The books also take place in areas of rapid change. Egypt, Palestine, the Sudan, and Haiti have all undergone many changes during the past two decades. Having picked a specific time frame, I could research and get the details right about what was going on in these places at that time. A few months earlier or later, and these places would look different. Such are the travails of placing a story in the real world.

Another big change right around this period was the world's embrace of cell phone technology. Silas avoids using cell phones because he says his unnamed enemy (Lucifer) might be able to intercept such messages. When Joseph summons him in Egypt, Silas steps to a pay phone, but, in fact, "calls" Joseph using a magic mirror. Charles uses his cell phone in Washington, but it is then disabled in the sea off Haiti. I am always aware of how authors use the technology of their period of their stories. Cell technology can greatly speed up the information flow between characters, and therefore move the story along quicker. I think I struck the right balance in telling this tale.

COULD THIS STORY HAVE HAPPENED?

One of the things I enjoy most about well told thrillers is the possibility that the story actually happened while no one was watching. *The Andromeda Strain*, *The Bourne Identity*, and *The DaVinci Code* (to cite three different genres of thriller) could all have happened, because by the end of the story, the heroes have mitigated any disaster that would have changed the world and been noticed by the rest of us. Any newsworthy events during the stories are plausibly absorbed by the normal flow of news. I think I have done that here as well. The nuclear attack off the coast of Georgia is averted. The British Navy would have retrieved their deactivated missile later without anyone ever knowing. (In fact, there was a suppressed news story around this time of the British Navy temporarily losing a nuke in the Atlantic.) The break-in at the British Museum, the blast on the Khartoum train, the fire in the Cairo office building, the bomb on the plane to Haiti, are all mundane daily violence in a violent, complacent world. Who can say these things didn't really happen in early 2001?

Another possibility that keeps coming back to me is what role Sammael, the Hebrew Demon Prince of Liars, played in the events of 9/11. Maybe Silas imprisoning him in April prevented him from taking action to prevent the Muslim attackers from destabilizing the pro-Jewish Western world. I'm sure I'm not the first occult writer to wonder about the involvement of mythological troublemakers like Sammael, or Ahriman, or the Coyote have played in our history of cruelty against one another.

SANANTHA THE DETECTIVE

Through all three of the books, Sanantha is the psychiatrist called in to help the protagonist. She is the nurturing anchor for these characters in turmoil. With her understanding of why people believe and act as they do, she is the right detective for the job. Marion Zimmer Bradley, the prolific fantasy author, once told me, "I don't want to read stories where the protagonist needs a cop or a lawyer. I want to read stories where the protagonist needs a psychiatrist or a priest." I concur.

Her background growing up in Haiti and being a practitioner of Voodoo gives her insights into the thread running through the series that Erzulie is Isis, and Isis is after Sammael who is Lucifer.

HUMAN CLONING IN 2004?

It takes months or years for scientific breakthroughs to make it through peer review, publication to journals, and then for summaries to appear in the popular press where the public sees them. Any discovery you read about today was cutting edge two or three years ago. By 2007, several labs had reported major breakthroughs in genetics including claims of cloning whole animals.

During *Goddess Daughter* in 2004, when Sanantha asks Randolph and Young Nae to explain their work, Young Nae is quick to accuse these rogue labs of falsifying data. (It turns out that they did, but I knew that, writing in the future.) Randolph's original work was the reconstruction of telomeres to reverse the aging of chromosomes. The products Young Nae markets are anti-aging creams. Randolph's big breakthrough, which had not been reviewed yet, was being able to substitute entire libraries of DNA into an organism using viruses, with the object of curing genetic diseases like Sickle Cell Anemia and Tay-Sachs disease. This technology was, in fact, perfected by 2010, since the successful results of ten-year trials came to light in 2020.

In *Goddess Daughter*, this technology is abused to accomplish cloning by substituting the father's half of a teenager's DNA with a copy of the mother's half, thus turning the daughter into a young copy of her mother. I set it up as a dynamic balancing act where the infecting slow virus does not kill the host, similar to Hantavirus, but rather pushes aside the replaced DNA and inserts itself symbiotically. I consulted with Dr. Susan Kane, a tumor biologist at the City of Hope, on my cloning protocol. She corrected some of my terminology, and said she appreciated what I was trying to do, even if my design is not really how these things work. That was good enough for me.

FUGU, MERIDIANS, AND DEATH TRAPS

Randolph's four-month memory gap is a carefully constructed trap to prevent him from remembering who committed the kidnapping and genetic raping of his daughter. I told you this story goes way dark.

The first layer of the trap is state-dependent memory. You can't recall where you parked your car after you've had a few drinks because your brain encoded the car's location with a sober set of brain chemicals. Those memories are not easily accessed if you have a different blood chemistry. This is also why cramming all night before a test does not work if you then get a couple of hours of sleep. What if you were poisoned with a powerful neurotoxin for months and then recovered? All the memories your brain encoded while stoned would be inaccessible when you are sober. What if you were poisoned with a drug that looks like you're just drunk and depressed, and no one suspects you've been poisoned? The drug tetrodotoxin is the poison in fugu pufferfish that is eaten as a thrill-seeking delicacy in Japan. It is also the main ingredient in the poison used to make people into work slaves in Haiti, *aka* Voodoo zombies. The villain of

Daughter Chosen learns of the poison because the story takes place in Malaysia where many Asian cultures are crammed next to each other. Sanantha Mauwad is able to identify the symptoms from her growing up in Haiti and seeing the effects halfway around the world.

Researching the preparation of fugu sushi (e.g., dedicated knives segregated from all the other utensils) and its use in zombie spells were fascinating rabbit holes to explore.

The second layer of the trap is much more sinister. *Chi* energy flows through the body along meridian pathways. *Kung fu* and *Tai chi chuan* teach users to move their *chi* on purpose. Traditional Medicine doctors invigorate key meridian points to enhance healing. The villain in this story did the opposite. By placing scars at key meridian points, they were able to link Randolph's heart to his brain in such a way that if he remembered what happened during his gap, his heart would stop.

The villain had their own reasons for not just killing Randolph, but rather only kill him if he managed to access those memories. We saw this first in *Goddess Chosen* when Silas talks about the Law of Necessity. When Sammael reaches for a nuclear option — literally, he commandeers a nuclear missile and fires it at Silas's ship — Silas knows his adversary is grasping at straws and will fail. Randolph's adversary also knows this subtle karmic principal and won't kill Randolph directly. Rather, they set a trap so that Randolph's own actions lead to his demise.

CHEONDOGYO, SILAT, AND CHI

I introduce additional functions of *chi* energy over the course of the first two books because, by *Goddess Rising*, I connect *chi* with other spiritual concepts to place magic in our world.

Young Nae Yoon was raised in the Korean religion of Cheondogyo, which teaches that each person has within them a portion of divine perfection. Korean culture is very family-oriented, and a central tenant of this faith is to respect everyone you meet and recognize the little bit of divinity that each of us has. Young Nae was rejected by his family and grew up a lone wolf. He has twisted the divine-self concept to justify his self-improvement as increasing the divinity within himself. He takes his business success, his physical prowess, even his ruthlessness as proof that the Divine is on his side.

Living in Malaysia, he learns esoteric forms of Silat, and uses his *chi* to dominate his opponents using their meridians against them. Eventually, he learns to move his killing energy beyond his touch and also into his voice. At that point, the reader starts to see how I have associated *chi* with magic. Randolph witnessing his friend's descent into darkness is one of the emotional cornerstones of *Goddess Daughter*.

DESIREE'S FALL AND SANANTHA'S INTERVENTION

All through the unraveling of the memory loss, the kidnapping, and the mystery of who the real villain is, Sanantha clings to her faith in Erzulie, her goddess of mercy, healing, and magic. Erzulie gives her clues which help, but are usually confusing, due to the nature of divine intervention. Principle among those is a vision of a snake doll inside a hollow child doll, nested inside a doll of a mother. She initially makes a wrong assumption about what it means, but eventually figures it out.

Poor Desiree. She goes with her father to her mother's funeral halfway around the world, is knocked out, and wakes up four months later, nude sun bathing in a jungle villa with no memories, strange color specks in her eyes, and a half an inch of jet black hair roots. She wanders the grounds and gets bitten by a snake and thinks she dies.

Through evil genetic manipulation, she was turned into a nineteen-year old clone of her mother Cheri, who had an affair with the villain. The villain even boasts that he brought his lover back from the dead. The cloning is a symbiotic dynamic relationship between the infecting virus with the mother-half genes, and her own body trying to restore its original genetic make-up. Remember state-dependent memory? When the virus is in full force, and she is 100% Cheri, her experiences are encoded and only accessible when she is 100% Cheri. When the virus is dormant, her father-half genes move back into place and she becomes Desiree again, gaining back her memories that were encoded while she was Desiree. It takes months for the transformation to complete due to the time it takes for cells to die and be replaced. So there are periods when Desiree has confusing mis-matched patches of memory, further adding to her horror.

When she is bitten by the snake in the jungle, the Cheri virus was mostly pushed into dormancy from months of sun-bathing, since viruses do not like ultraviolet light. The snake bite kills her. Yep, stops her breathing and she dies. But the virus is still alive. And the virus steps in, swaps itself into her DNA, and restarts her systems. At that point, she is a virus in human form — a person with no soul.

When Randolph and Sanantha find her, he tries to take advantage of a penicillin allergy that Cheri has, but Desiree does not. Even worse, Randolph is faced with his wife apparently returned from the dead. He must choose between getting his wife back and saving his daughter. Sanantha reminds him this is not really Cheri, but a highly unstable illusion. He chooses to save Desiree. He kills the Cheri virus, hoping the Desiree identity can re-emerge. But he doesn't know Desiree died of a snake bite.

As she passes away for the last time, Sanantha makes one last desperate appeal to Erzulie to take pity on this poor victimized child ... and the goddess does.

We later see that Erzulie, who is Isis, had her eye on Desiree all along. Sanantha suspects Sammael may have tried to ruin Erzulie's her plan by sending a snake to kill her. We know it wasn't Sammael, because we know that in 2004 Sammael was in the pocket universe prison built by Silas Alverado at the end of *Goddess Chosen*. Seeing the girl lose her soul, Isis acted boldly and possessed her.

7

THE GRAND ARC COMES TOGETHER

AVENGERS ASSEMBLE

I N *GODDESS CHOSEN*, ISIS REINCARNATES her old High Priest to be her champion to capture Sammael. He succeeds (spoiler), but does not get Lucifer to hand over the Tablets of Aeth. In *Goddess Daughter*, Isis finds a young woman who has lost her soul in a cloning disaster, and the goddess possesses her as an avatar on Earth. In *Goddess Rising*, Isis realizes Sammael has escaped and is too slippery, so she has her avatar assemble a team of supernatural beings to finally get the job done.

By the third book, *Goddess Rising*, I have established that *chi* energy is the soul, and that mages and angels (fallen and otherwise) wield this energy as magic. To tell the concluding story, I needed to show Sammael's true motivation throughout the whole series: his obsession with wiping out the Egyptian pantheon. He sees them as an abomination because those gods see themselves as independent of his God. He has tried repeatedly throughout history to do this. First was his sabotage of Exodus in ancient Egypt. He wasn't satisfied with God's plan to free the Hebrews, he wanted to cripple the worship of the Egyptian gods. He probably tried again during Roman times by influencing key figures who made sure Egypt was conquered. But the gods had been adopted and reborn across the globe. The West Africans who were stolen to the Americas took their versions. These are the Voodouns that Silas wants to convert. Sammael couldn't let that happen, so we have the conflict in *Goddess Chosen*. The old gods also made their way across Europe and were reborn again in ancient Ireland.

SAINT PATRICK AND THE DEVIL

Desiree Macklin recovers from her cloning, goes back to college, and graduates four years later with a degree in Art History. She hasn't been sick a day in four years and she may have some lay-of-the-hands healing powers. She used her time in college to research the world's religions and their history, trying to figure out what happened to her when Sanantha asked Erzulie to save her life. She travels to Ireland to check out her Irish roots and meets a young ghostbuster named Alec Doogan. They share notes on spirituality, and he takes her on an expedition to the site of Saint Patrick's grave. Using his condenser fluid, the recipe of which he found in ancient texts, they find the actual grave which had been lost over time and myth. The grave carries Saint Patrick's soul signature, but also another even more powerful signature. Saint Patrick is said to have been visited and guided by angels, so they are left thinking they have uncovered proof of the angel in the fluid-enhanced Kirlian soul residue image.

Desiree also meets Joseph from *Goddess Chosen*. He recognizes that she is walking around with a soul given by his goddess. He warns her that her ghostbusting with Alec will put her in danger.

As I was researching the components I would need to pit Lucifer against the Celtic gods (as the last inheritors of his sworn enemies the Egyptians), I uncovered another wonderful coincidence, much like discovering how Ramses switched High Priests when I needed it for my story. I uncovered a myth of how Saint Patrick confronted the Druid elders and defeated them in supernatural combat. We're talking Old Testament bringing down hellfire stuff. And he did it after converting a local youth as his acolyte, a fellow named Benen. The myth says Patrick warned the Druids that, if they did not admit that his God was the only God, then his God would strike them down. A Druid priest stepped up and challenged Patrick, at which point the fellow was flung high into the air and smashed to death. The druids withdrew and came back the next night, demanding further proof. Patrick put his acolyte Benen in a wooden shed with a Druid lad, and burned the building to the ground. Benen emerged unscathed. The Druid king relented and had his people convert. Benin went on be very influential in Patrick's spread of Christianity across Ireland. Benin was eventually canonized as Saint Benignus, and he is celebrated today.

Sound familiar? Insinuate yourself into a conflict with your old enemies and throw around some magic to make sure they are utterly defeated. Yes, in my telling of the tale, Benen was Sammael in disguise, just as Faenka/Nebwnenef was also him in disguise.

Joseph is suspicious of this myth, so he goes to Tara Hill, to the Stone of Destiny where this is supposed to have happened. Joseph's powers derive from his being an archangel of his god Ptah, who is the Opener of the Ways. Hence, Joseph's powers are primarily in his eyes. He can see the truth of whatever he is looking at, which includes what happened to an object in the past. He communes with the stone and sees its past as a way to time travel in his mind's eye. He sees that the stone used to be further up the valley in a highlands some miles away. From there, he "witnesses" the events of Patrick's conflict those fateful nights so long ago.

After 5th century Ireland, Sammael thought he had finally wiped them out. But their influence lived on in West Africa, and eventually was brought to the Caribbean by the slave trade a thousand years later. When Sammael tries to stop Silas and his Voodoo plans, Silas epically insults him by capturing him in a magical Egyptian prison. When he escapes eight years later, he is furious and all the more determined to end them.

DESIREE THE AVATAR

Desiree has spent four years looking for answers and Joseph has them. Sanantha does not trust Joseph at all, and she flies to Ireland to keep Desiree safe. During the years after Desiree's rebirth, Sanantha has been her counselor and became her friend. Technically, she did save Desiree's life. Joseph explains that Desiree has the soul of his goddess, and she should have a connection. Alec tests Desiree's life signature and finds she has the *chi* of at least six people. She explores this with Joseph's guidance and finds she has healing powers. She also finds that when the goddess wants her to do something, she really cannot resist. More than once, the goddess forces Desiree to look at something or follow something with Desiree not knowing what she is pursuing until the goddess's plan becomes clear.

One such instance is Alec's OCD. Alec is quite compulsive and often has trouble coping with crowds and outdoor spaces. He takes a form of serotonin to help moderate his reactions. Sammael progressively lowers his dosage (we'll talk about how in a moment) and Alec becomes increasing tense and unstable. Sammael wants to make him more malleable to suggestion. Isis sees this and pushes Desiree to do a laying of hands. Desiree can visualize that something is broken in his brain, but has no idea what she is seeing. The goddess does, and heals him. Sammael is disappointed when he finds out his ruse did not work.

MICHAEL

A government revenue agent named Michael Archbald shows up, investigating Benito's finances. An FBI agent named Jill Bitterman shows up chasing the same terrorist who killed so many people in Washington, D.C. eight years earlier at the end of *Goddess Chosen*. Jill is one of my favorite characters. Raised Southern Baptist, but done with church politics, she should look somewhat familiar to fans of *The X-Files*. She reads the Bible every night before bed, and is about as determined and capable a field agent as you could want on your side.

Oh, Agent Archibald is actually the archangel Michael, the one who threw Sammael out of heaven. I had a lot of fun writing their brotherly interactions. Michael forms a tense, but focused, working relationship with Joseph, who is an archangel of the Egyptian pantheon. Although all three of these angels use different tactics and manifest their magic in different forms, they all use the same energy, which is identified as the energy of the soul or Holy Spirit.

THE DEVIL IN THEIR MIDST

To tell this story correctly, I needed to show the reader Sammael's motives. I admit, I had a lot of fun writing Lucifer as a character. I also had a lot of fun engineering situations where the other characters remained oblivious to his identity while the reader is cringing at his continued success.

In *Goddess Daughter*, I was careful to keep the true identity of the villain hidden from the reader and the characters until it became clear that everything you see in the first half of the book turns out to be deception. In *Goddess Rising*, I show you the Devil on Page One.

He adopts the persona of Benito Nomini, befriends Alec, manages to never cross paths with Joseph (who can see the truth), and seduces Sanantha. He backs Alec's work both financially and by giving him artifacts and spell books. In short order, Alec has moved from detecting spirits to commanding them. The magic he wields looks a lot like the magic we saw Silas wield in *Goddess Chosen*. Despite Sanantha's and Desiree's warning, Alec becomes quite seduced by the power.

Benito films Alec performing magic and posts it on social media without asking Alec. The videos go viral, which further seduces Alec to go public. He performs a small public miracle by freezing a fountain, and his following explodes. Benito takes him to the driest desert on Earth and has Alec summon rain. Benito films the whole thing, with Sanantha in Africa and Desiree manning the servers back in Ireland. Midway through the spell, Benito shuts down the experiment, giving only a flimsy excuse that it was going too fast and the audience would think it was faked. We later find out moving that much water creates static electricity that manifests as lightning. Again, I work the magic in with the science to make it believable. Getting the science right means doing the research.

OM MANI PADME HUM

Meanwhile, Joseph teaches Desiree how to channel her god soul energy to do things only angels can usually do, like travel between this world and the spirit plane. Joseph explains to Desiree that holy sites are where the separation between this plane and the spirit plane is thin and can be traversed. When he shows her how he does this, she recognizes his pose as the sideways stance found in Egyptian pictographs. He says that art style was popular because people wanted to be portrayed as if they knew angelic secrets. Desiree, who has a degree in religious art, is amazed that no one has ever deduced this.

Isis gives Desiree a vision of being the Celestial Dragon collecting the pearl that is "the Jewel that Grants All Wishes", the Om Mani Padme Hum. Joseph takes her to Tibet using his teleportation. They enlist a monk named Renpo. who recognizes them having supernatural souls. By the way, there actually are two temples in Purang, Nepal with competing philosophies about defending Buddhism. They visit Mount Kailash and gate to the spirit realm. In that plane, the mountain is Mount Sumeru, the center of the universe. They follow clues from myths and find the Pearl. I had so much fun researching and tying Buddhist lore into this sequence. The Pearl allows its holder to not only see the truth, the way Joseph can, but the entire story, stripped of all ego, assumptions, and deception (fulfillment of the Buddha's vison). Needless to say, this is a very powerful weapon against the Prince of Liars.

Renpo teaches Desiree *tai chi chuan* so she can focus her god soul *chi* into action. He teaches her everything he knows over the last half of the book. This includes special senses that are activated by manipulating *chi* energies. *Tai chi* was fascinating to research. I will definitely be going back to that trough. With the soul of the goddess, she is able to achieve deeper, more powerful results than he expects. He pushes her until she can achieve *satori*, that state of enlightened no-self that allows perfect concentration and complete command of her godlike abilities. Their hope is with this improved perception and reaction time, she will be able to deal with whatever Sammael throws at her.

CLEVER DEVIL

With the Pearl, two archangels, and satori-focused god energy, you would think Desiree would be ready to tackle Sammael. But the Devil has been busy. Just before going into battle, Desiree loses both Joseph and Michael. And she still hasn't figured out who Sammael is or how he will attack. Sanantha is useless, busy being smitten with her lover Benito. And Alec is caught up with becoming an Internet famous magician. All my research on Catholicism, Buddhism, Egypt — all those details are the clockwork that moves into place for the final confrontation. Lining up the ancient Celtic gods with the Egyptian pantheon is the last piece of the puzzle. Just when all appears lost, a quietly forgotten Catholic saint puts in her helping hand by turning a rather esoteric key that Desiree collected from the spirit realm version of the Temple of Isis at Philae.

Sammael's final bow is revealed when he has utterly defamed the Egyptian gods and is about to succeed in driving away the last of their followers, Desiree pleads with her follow gods to intervene, but they tell her the magic Sammael gave Alec was not theirs, but a twisted version of Sammael's creation. This is exactly what Sammael did to the Egyptians in Exodus. He showed them magic and told them it was the same as what Moses was wielding, but it was actually a lie of his own design.

WHAT NEXT?

At the end of *Goddess Rising* (spoilers), Isis has finished her quest, and Desiree is left with powers derived from the goddess, but no longer driven by the goddess's heavy hand. Joseph, Sanantha, and Renpo are all by her side. She says she is there for the believers in their faith. Algis Budrys, science fiction author and one of the founders of *The Writers of the Future*, said that a satisfying story is one that ends by giving the reader permission to leave the story and go back to their lives. This ending does that.

Could Desiree, nascent goddess, have more adventures? Of course. These stories are set in 2001, 2004, and 2009. In keeping with that pattern, I could set the next one in 2011 thru 2013 and have it focus on how Desiree defends the re-emerging Egyptian faith during the Arab Spring in Libya and Egypt. Maybe Silas finds a way to bring Ramses the Great back to Earth, and he and Desiree, the embodiment of his goddess, have a showdown. Maybe.

8

THANK YOU

THERE YOU HAVE IT. Three books full of fantasy and science fiction details that unfold at thriller speed, but which have all been carefully researched from facts in our world. My challenge was to tell an engrossing story about revenge, redemption, loss, forgiveness, and justice, that encourages the reader to think about how disparate details can fit together and reveal a world usually hidden from view.

To those of you who have read the books first, thank you. I hope this treatise has helped you enjoy them more.

To those of you who have not read the books, but read this volume first, I hope I have not given away too many spoilers, but rather intrigued you into wanting to dive into the books now.

Enjoy them in good health!

ABOUT THE AUTHOR

Jay Hartlove is the award-winning author of the urban fantasy "Goddess Rising" trilogy (*Goddess Chosen, Goddess Daughter,* and *Goddess Rising*), the fantasy romance *Mermaid Steel*, and the science fiction thriller *The Insane God*. He is also the playwright, director and producer of *The Mirror's Revenge*, the musical sequel to the "Snow White" fable, which had its theatrical run in the San Francisco Bay Area in August 2018 to rave reviews.

His stories are filled with conspiracies and the supernatural, gods, dreams, angels, and hidden connections. His creative motto is "Dark Secrets Revealed". He loves to take stories where the reader does not expect, with sympathetic villains, heroes with very dark pasts, and lots of plot twists. He turns victims into heroes. He was selected as one of the "50 Authors You Should Be Reading" by *The Authors Show.*

Jay is a former competitive costumer, having won Best in Show at both San Diego ComicCon and WorldCon. You can read more about Jay's creative adventures, including much of the research he put into his books, at *jaywrites.com.*

"GODDESS RISING" TRILOGY

GODDESS CHOSEN

BOOK ONE OF THE "GODDESS RISING" TRILOGY

The man who would beat the devil isn't a hero, but a ruthless madman.

GODDESS DAUGHTER

BOOK TWO OF THE "GODDESS RISING" TRILOGY

How far can you genetically alter someone before she becomes someone else ... before she loses her soul?

GODDESS RISING

BOOK THREE OF THE "GODDESS RISING" TRILOGY

Saved by a goddess ... but only as a tool for revenge?

Available from Water Dragon Publishing in
hardcover, trade paperback, digital, and audio editions
waterdragonpublishing.com

ALSO BY JAY HARTLOVE

THE INSANE GOD

A meteorite fragment cures a teenaged trans girl's schizophrenia, but leaves her with visions of ancient warring gods annihilating each other in space.

MERMAID STEEL

The power of love over hate.

A grand adventure, a hero with a dark past, a powerful goddess, and a message of hope for us all.

Available from Water Dragon Publishing in
hardcover, trade paperback, digital, and audio editions
waterdragonpublishing.com

www.ingramcontent.com/pod-product-compliance
Lightning Source LLC
Chambersburg PA
CBHW031036190726
48286CB00003BA/1202